MAJESTIC HORSES

SHETLAND PONIES

by Pamela Dell

The Child's World

Published in the United States of America by The Child's World®
PO Box 326 • Chanhassen, MN 55317-0326
800-599-READ • www.childsworld.com

PHOTO CREDITS
© Ace Stock Limited/Alamy: 26
© blickwinkel/Alamy: 8, 21
© Doug Houghton/Alamy: cover, 1, 7
© General Photographic Agency/Hulton Archive/Getty Images: 19
© Gourlay Steell/The Bridgeman Art Library/Getty Images: 16
© Jeremy Pardoe/Alamy: 15
© Juniors Bildarchiv/Alamy: 25
© SuperStock/Alamy: 23
© The Photolibrary Wales/Alamy: 11
© Ute & Jürgen Schimmelpfennig/zefa/Corbis: 4

ACKNOWLEDGMENTS
The Child's World®: Mary Berendes, Publishing Director;
Katherine Stevenson, Editor

Content Adviser: Weezee

The Design Lab: Kathleen Petelinsek, Design and Page Production

LIBRARY OF CONGRESS CATALOGING-IN-PUBLICATION DATA
Dell, Pamela.
  Shetland ponies / by Pamela Dell.
    p. cm. — (Majestic horses)
  Includes bibliographical references and index.
  ISBN 1-59296-785-X (library bound : alk. paper)
  1. Shetland pony—Juvenile literature. I. Title. II. Series.
  SF315.2.S5D45 2007
  636.1'6—dc22   2006022648

TABLE OF CONTENTS

Hardy Little Ponies. 5

What Do Shetland Ponies Look Like?. . . .6

Newborn Shetland Ponies. 13

Shetland Ponies in History. 14

What Are Shetland Ponies Like?. 20

Shetland Ponies at Work. 22

Shetland Ponies Today. 24

Body Parts of a Horse. 28

Glossary. 30

To Find Out More 31

Index. 32

★ ★ ★ HARDY LITTLE PONIES

The Shetland Islands lie in the stormy seas north of Scotland. The islands are rocky and hilly. Life there is hard. Cold winds blow for much of the year. Rough waves pound the shore. Often, the land is covered with thick mist.

Shetland ponies are sometimes called "shelties."

But people live in this cold, lonely place. So do some very small horses. The horses are called Shetland ponies. They have lived on the islands for well over a thousand years. Ponies of this **breed** are strong and **hardy**. People around the world love them as pets and show horses.

◀ This Shetland pony lives on a Shetland Islands farm.

WHAT DO SHETLAND PONIES LOOK LIKE?

Many Shetland ponies are shorter than you are! Like all horses, their height is measured at the **withers**. These ponies are less than 42 inches (106 centimeters) tall. Many of them are much shorter. **Miniature** Shetland ponies are really small. Some of them are only 32 inches (81 centimeters) tall!

Shetland ponies are sturdy and stocky. They often weigh about 300 to 500 pounds (140 to 230 kilograms). Their bodies are round and full. Their legs are short and strong. Their heads are small and well shaped.

Shetland ponies are the smallest pure breed of horse in the world. Some horses are smaller, but they are a mix of breeds.

This Shetland pony has a small, powerful body. It also has a thick coat that keeps it warm. ▶

The Shetland Islands are cold, windy, and wet. But Shetland ponies do well there. In the summer, their coat is short, shiny, and smooth. But for winter, they grow a thick coat to stay warm. Special "guard" hairs keep their skin from getting wet. Their bodies lose little heat.

The pony's thick mane and tail also help in bad weather. The mane covers the pony's head and neck. The pony's long **forelock** keeps its face warm and dry. Even the ears have long, soft hair. The hair keeps out rain and snow.

Shetland ponies' long tails often drag on the ground. In winter, Shetlands sometimes get snowballs on their tails! Icicles hang from their hair, too.

◄ You can see this Shetland pony's long, thick mane and forelock. All that hair helps keep the pony's head and ears warm.

Shetland ponies are most often black or dark brown. They can be many other colors, too. Some of them have big patches of white. This patchy coloring is called **piebald**. But Shetland ponies are never spotted.

People brought Shetland ponies to North America over a hundred years ago. Over time, some of these ponies were mixed with other breeds. This mixing made a new, different American breed. These newer American Shetlands are not as round and stocky.

Shetland ponies have big **nostrils**. On the Shetland Islands, big nostrils helped warm the cold air.

These Shetland ponies live on a farm in Wales. Their owners have given them hay to eat. ▶

★ ★ ★ NEWBORN SHETLAND PONIES

Foals grow very thick coats in the winter. In spring, the hair hangs in long clumps, then falls off. Brushing helps get rid of the clumps.

Mares of many horse breeds have a **foal** every year. But Shetland pony mares have a foal every two years. The newborn foals are no bigger than many stuffed animals! They are usually less than 23 inches (58 centimeters) tall. They might be small, but they are hardy. In the Shetland Islands, even the foals live outside. Their thick coats help keep them warm.

Shetland foals often seem to prefer small people. They might act shy or nervous around adults. But they often walk right up to children. Getting used to people helps them become friendly pets.

◄ This Shetland pony has legs almost as long as its mother's! Its body will fill out as it gets older.

★ SHETLAND PONIES IN HISTORY

No one is sure where Shetland ponies first came from. No one is sure how they got to the Shetland Islands. But they have been on the islands for a very long time. Early pictures from the islands show small horses. These pictures are about 1,200 years old. They were carved in stone. They show people riding well-built little ponies.

Early Shetland ponies were strong and sturdy. They could do more than just carry people. They could haul heavy loads. People on the islands put them to work.

Viking sailors came to the Shetland Islands during the 800s. Some people think Shetland ponies came from the Vikings' small horses.

People of long ago would have seen a sight much like this one. This Shetland pony is walking on a hill on the Shetland Islands. ▶

16

Life on the islands was hard. The farmers used seaweed to help their crops grow. They needed fuel to heat their homes. The ponies helped them move these things. The ponies pulled wagons and carried big packs. They also pulled plows. They spent all their time living outside—in any weather. They became known for doing extra-hard work.

Long ago, children worked hard in English coal mines. In 1847, a law stopped children from doing that work. Ponies took the children's place.

In the mid-1800s, lots of Shetland ponies were taken to England. People wanted them to work in coal mines. The ponies were small. They could work in the narrow tunnels. The ponies lived underground. They pulled cartloads of coal year after year. Over time, machines took the ponies' place.

◀ This painting is from the 1800s. It shows a wealthy boy in Scotland. The Shetland pony was his pet.

People brought Shetland ponies to North America, too. Some of the ponies worked in American coal mines. People also wanted them as riding horses. And they wanted them for pulling riders in carts.

By the 1920s and 1930s, people seemed to forget about Shetland ponies. They kept other breeds as pets. They no longer needed the ponies for working. Few people seemed to care about keeping the breed alive. But over time, people became interested again. Today, Shetland ponies have made a big comeback!

In the Shetland Islands, ponies were very important. Even their mane and tail hair was used in fishing nets and lines. Cutting the mane or tail of someone else's pony was against the law.

This picture shows a pony at work on the Shetland Islands. It is helping the farmer carry heavy loads. ▶

WHAT ARE SHETLAND PONIES LIKE?

For their size, Shetland ponies are very strong! And they are very hardy. They can work hard, but they also make excellent pets. That is why so many people like them.

Shetland ponies are quick learners. They are smart, friendly, and lively. They can also be trusted. Their gentle nature makes them good for people with special needs. They are great choices for kids just learning to ride. Many kids learn to ride on Shetlands. Often, they do not want to switch to bigger horses!

Shetland ponies seem to love the snow. After a deep snowfall, they run and chase each other. Like children, they often kick up their legs and roll in the snow.

This girl is riding her Shetland pony. She and the pony are good friends. She does not even need a saddle. ▶

SHETLAND PONIES AT WORK

In earlier times, Shetland ponies worked hard. Today, they no longer work in coal mines or farm fields. Their jobs are easier—and more fun! Many of them are kept just as pets. People ride them for fun and in horse shows.

Many Shetland ponies also take part in **contests**. People use them for racing and jumping. They enter them in weight-pulling contests, too. Wherever they go, Shetland ponies are crowd pleasers!

Sometimes groups of Shetland ponies work in teams. They pull small carts or wagons in shows and parades.

This Shetland pony has been trained to jump over low bars. ▶

★ ★ ★ SHETLAND PONIES TODAY

Lots of people are working to help the Shetland pony breed. Many people belong to Shetland pony clubs. Through careful planning, these clubs help keep the breed pure. They keep Shetlands from getting mixed with other breeds.

Some of the best Shetland ponies still come from the Shetland Islands. But they live in many other countries, too. In fact, they are found all over the world.

There is a separate club for American Shetland ponies. That is because they are a different breed.

This Shetland pony's mane blows as it runs in a meadow. ▶

Shetland ponies live longer than many other horses. Many live into their twenties. One Shetland pony born in Germany lived to be 50!

Few breeds have been around as long as the Shetland pony. Few breeds are as strong or as hardy. And no breed has worked harder!

But today, Shetlands do not have to work so hard for a living. Instead, people can enjoy them as pets. These shaggy little ponies have won friends all over the world.

◄ These Shetland ponies are good friends. They nuzzle each other to say hello.

★ ★ ★ BODY PARTS OF A HORSE

1. Ears
2. Forelock
3. Forehead
4. Eyes
5. Nostril
6. Lips
7. Muzzle
8. Chin
9. Cheek
10. Neck
11. Shoulder
12. Chest
13. Forearm
14. Knee
15. Cannon
16. Coronet
17. Hoof

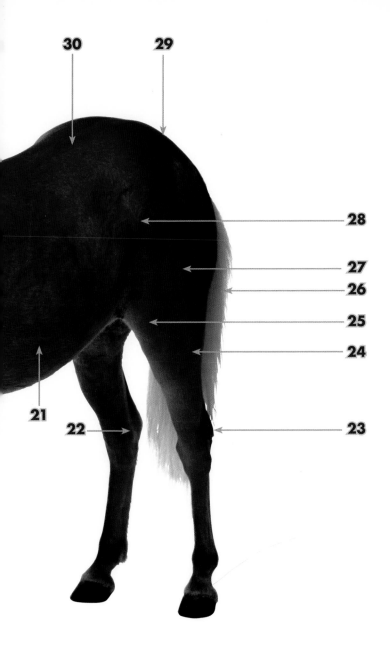

18. Pastern
19. Fetlock
20. Elbow
21. Barrel
22. Chestnut
23. Hock
24. Gaskin
25. Stifle
26. Tail
27. Thigh
28. Point of hip
29. Croup
30. Loin
31. Back
32. Withers
33. Mane
34. Poll

GLOSSARY

breed (BREED) A breed is a certain type of an animal. Shetland ponies are a breed of small horse.

contests (KAHN-tests) In contests, people or animals try to win by being the best at something. People enter Shetland ponies in different kinds of contests.

foal (FOHL) A foal is a baby horse. Shetland pony foals are very small.

forelock (FOR-lock) A horse's forelock is the hair that grows out of its forehead. Shetland ponies' forelocks help keep them warm.

hardy (HAR-dee) Hardy means able to stay alive under hard conditions. Shetland ponies are small but hardy.

mares (MAIRZ) Mares are female horses. Shetland pony mares have a baby every other year.

miniature (MIN-ee-uh-chur) Miniature means small for its kind. Miniature Shetland ponies are smaller than other Shetlands.

nostrils (NOS-trulz) Nostrils are the openings in an animal's nose through which it breathes or smells. Shetland ponies have big nostrils.

piebald (PY-bald) A piebald animal has big patches of color. Some Shetland ponies are piebald.

withers (withers) The withers is the highest part of a horse's back. A Shetland pony's height is measured at the withers.

TO FIND OUT MORE

In the Library

Cannan, Joanna. Hamish: *The Story of a Shetland Pony.*
Wiltshire (UK): Cavalier Paperbacks, 1995.

Clover, Peter. *Sheltie the Shetland Pony.* London (UK): Puffin, 2002.

Yolen, Jane, and William Stobbs. *Greyling: A Picture Story from the Shetland Islands.*
Cleveland, OH: Collins & World, 1975.

On the Web

Visit our Web site for lots of links about Shetland ponies:
http://www.childsworld.com/links

Note to Parents, Teachers, and Librarians: We routinely check our Web links
to make sure they're safe, active sites—so encourage your readers to check them out!

INDEX

American Shetland
    ponies, 10, 24
appearance, 6, 9, 10, 13

babies, 13

coat, 9, 13
colors, 10
contests, 22

England, 17

foals, 13
forelock, 9

hands (height), 6

history, 5, 10, 14, 17, 18
horse shows, 22

jumping, 22

life span, 27

mane, 9, 18
mares, 13
miniature Shetland
    ponies, 6

North America, 10, 18

personality, 13, 20
as pets, 5, 13, 20, 22, 27

piebald, 10
popularity, 18, 22, 27

racing, 22

Scotland, 5
Shetland Islands, 5, 9, 13,
    14, 17, 18, 24

tail, 9, 18

Vikings, 14

withers, 6
working, 14, 17, 18, 22, 27

About the author: Pamela Dell is the author of more than fifty books for young people. She likes writing about four-legged animals as well as insects, birds, famous people, and interesting times in history. She has published both fiction and nonfiction books and has also created several interactive computer games for kids. Pamela divides her time between Los Angeles, where the weather is mostly warm and sunny all year, and Chicago, where she loves how wildly the seasons change every few months.